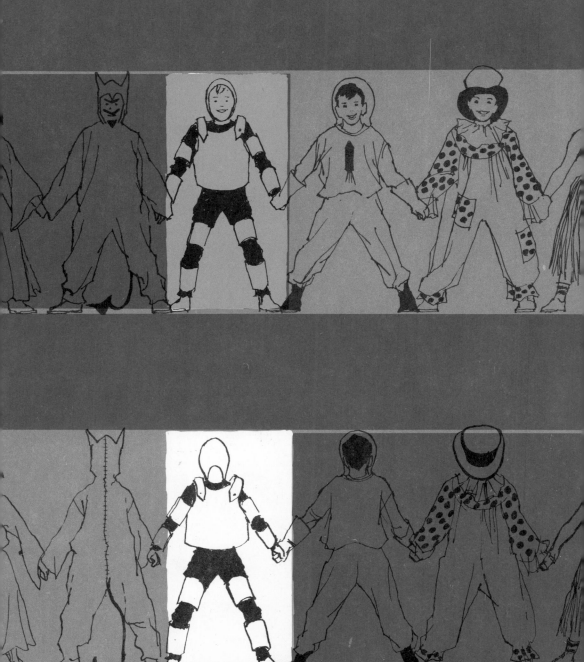

Sir Halloween

JERROLD BEIM

Illustrated by
Tracy Sugarman

ILLIAM MORROW & COMP███████████ 1959

One Saturday morning Randy
went downtown with his father
and mother. "Look!" He stopped
in front of a store window.
"Pumpkins, witches, masks! Halloween is coming soon."

"That's right," Dad said. "It's always the last night of October."

"Halloween is coming!" Everyone started to talk about it in school.

"What are you going to be?"
Randy asked his best friend Mike.
"I don't know," Mike said.
"Last year I was a pirate. Maybe

I'll be a tramp this year. What
are you going to be?"

"I don't know," Randy said.
"But something good."

Randy thought and thought about what he wanted to be. A clown? No, he had been a clown once, when he was a little boy. A fat man, all stuffed with pillows and wearing his father's suit? No, that wasn't good enough. A ghost in a sheet? No, he had seen one once and wasn't scared at all!

Every Monday evening Randy
watched a television show about
knights in armor. Tonight two
knights were having a fierce battle.
Clang, clang, clang! went their
swords. And suddenly Randy knew

what he wanted to be on Halloween—a knight in armor.

As soon as the program ended,
he ran to Mom. "I'm going to be
a knight in armor on Halloween,"
he said.

"A knight in armor!" Mom exclaimed. "That's a good idea, Randy, but the costume would be too expensive."

"We don't have to buy it," Randy said. "We can make it. We can put shiny tin foil over cardboard for the top part and use tin cans for my arms and legs."

"Well, I'm willing to try it if you think it will work," Mom agreed.

Randy didn't tell anybody about
his plans, except Mike. "That
sounds great!" Mike said.

Randy started making his costume right away. He made a big
sword out of wood and painted it

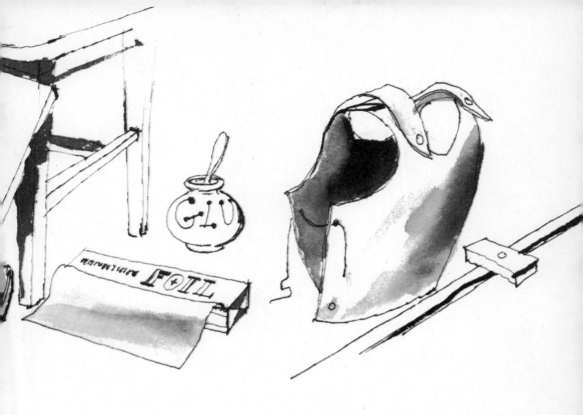

silver. He used the top of a crate
for a shield and painted lions on
it. He found large pieces of cardboard and cut the back and front
of his armor out of them. Then
he glued shiny foil on them and
wired them together.

His mother had collected four tin cans so far. He cut out their tops and bottoms and put one can on each arm and each leg. When he stood in front of a mirror, he wasn't sure he looked like a knight in armor. I'll look better when I get some more tin cans, he thought.

But Randy still didn't know what he was going to wear on his head. He and his mother watched the television show again. "I could knit you a helmet," his mother said. "I'll use gray wool so it will look as if it were made of metal."

Television

It was getting nearer and nearer to Halloween. Everybody would go from door to door early in the evening. Then at seven-thirty they would go to a big party at school. Prizes were going to be given for the best costumes. "I hope I win!" Randy said.

A few days before Halloween Randy went downtown again. He bought a silver mask to wear with his costume. Mom bought lots of candy to give to the boys and girls who came to the house.

And then it was Halloween!
Everyone was so excited that they
hardly worked in school at all.
Randy was afraid it might rain,
but when night came the stars

were shining brightly. While he
was eating dinner, the doorbell
rang. A group of little boys and
girls had come trick-or-treating.
Randy gave them all some candy.

Now it was time for him to get dressed. He put on his suit of armor and the knitted helmet. Mom and Dad said the costume was perfect.

"Lend me your sword a minute and kneel in front of me," Dad said. "I now dub you Sir Halloween."

Just then there was a knock at the door.

It was Mike, dressed as a tramp. "You look wonderful!" he said to Randy.

"You look good too," Randy said.

"I'll drive you to the school party when you come back," Dad said.

Down the street went the tramp
and the knight. They met an old
lady, a space man, and Little Red
Ridinghood. They guessed that
Red Ridinghood was a girl named
Mary Smith, but they didn't know

who the others were. And nobody
could guess who *they* were.

Then they went to a house and
rang the doorbell. "Trick or treat,"
they said. The lady gave them
some candy bars.

Down the street they went to more houses. They met Robin Hood, two pirates, and a devil. At some houses they were given candy and cookies. One lady gave them each ten cents. At the next house, the door opened quickly. "Trick or tr—" Randy started to say, but then he stopped in surprise.

Another knight stood in front of him! Randy knew the boy who lived in this house, because he went to the same school.

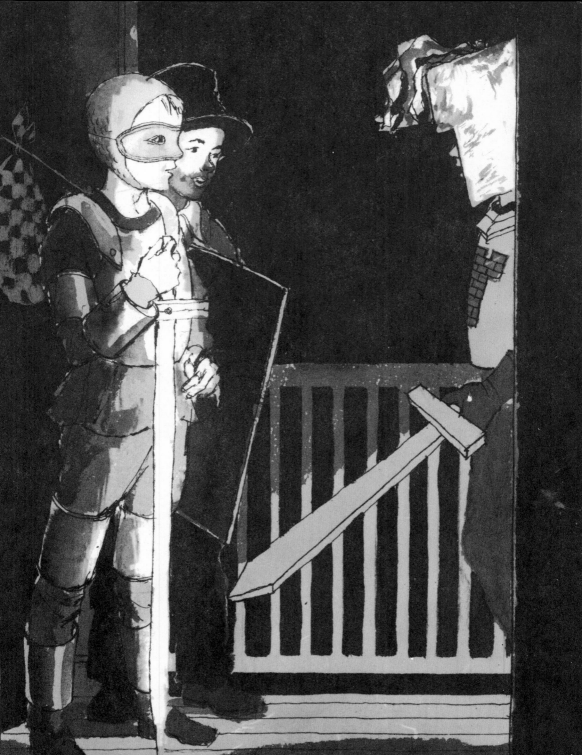

"Don't worry," Mike whispered
to Randy. "I think your costume
is better. You'll win the prize at
school."

Randy tried not to feel bad. He
hoped it wouldn't matter if there

was another knight. They went to
another house and collected some
more treats. On their way to the
next house they heard a rattling
sound. They turned and saw another knight!

"Let's . . . let's go back to my house," Randy said.

"Yes, we know," Dad said, when he opened the door and saw Randy's sad face. "Some of those other knights came here. But you look the best of all."

"But I thought I'd win a prize," Randy said. "I wish I could change my costume for the party."

"It's too late to do that," Mom answered. "Don't worry. You'll have fun anyway, even if you don't win a prize."

The school party was held in
the gym. Lots of boys and girls
were already there in many kinds
of costumes. But Randy felt worse
than ever. Everywhere he looked

he saw another knight!

There were many games to play, like biting apples on a string and throwing beanbags into a hole. But Randy didn't want to play.

Finally an important announce-
ment came. "Line up for the Grand
Parade!"

And then as Randy looked at
all the other knights again, he
suddenly had an idea.

Quickly he talked to one knight
and then to another. Soon he had
talked to them all.

Now the big parade before the
judges began. Everyone clapped
when the boy dressed up like a
kangaroo hopped across the floor.
Some people thought the girl
dressed like Cinderella at the ball
was good. And then someone
cried, "Look what's coming now!"

An army of knights was march-
ing in two straight lines through
the door. When they were all in
the gym, they stopped to have a
fierce, make-believe battle with
their swords and shields.

Everyone shouted and clapped and whistled. The crowd had never seen such an exciting parade before.

The parade was over now, and the judges started talking together to decide on the prizes. They hardly took a minute to make up their minds. "First prize goes to the battling knights," the head judge announced.

The prize was a big box of candy,
and the knights sent Randy up to
take it for them. They gave him

the first candy from the box, too.
After all, it had been Randy's idea
to have them all march together.

Randy smiled happily in the
midst of the excited knights. This
Halloween had turned out to be
the best of all.